I'd Rather Be With You

by

Kay Shanee

Kay Shanee

ABOUT THE AUTHOR

Kay is a forty-something wife and mother, born and raised in the Midwest. During the day, she is a high school teacher and track coach. In her free time, she enjoys spending time with her family and friends. Her favorite pastime is reading and writing romance novels about the dopeness of BLACK LOVE.

DEDICATION

My husband is my inspiration. He supports me in every way and that means everything. I laugh when I think of when I was explaining this storyline to him. He wasn't paying attention and thought I was talking about real people. I'm sure this is somebody's story, I just don't know them. Thanks for listening, baby. I love you, always and forever!

SYNOPSIS

Keva Jamison has lusted after her brother's best friend, Damarion, for years. When they finally hook up, her lust turned love consumes her thoughts and all that she can think about is being with him. The dilemma…Keva has a man and doesn't know how to tell him that she'd rather be with someone else.

Damarion Sanders is the ultimate bachelor and in no rush to settle down. He's been in a situationship for several months but only because he can't have who he really desires. But after succumbing to his attraction to Keva, his best friend's sister, making her his forever is the only thing on his mind, except…he promised his best friend that he'd stay away from Keva.

Will Keva and Damarion find a way to be together? Will Keva risk her relationship and take a chance on giving Damarion all of her love? Will Damarion break the promise he made to his best friend and risk eighteen years of friendship for the woman he's come to love?

A Poem for Keva

You are, the best part of me
My in between
My parts unseen
My intimacy – damn Keva
I never felt like this about anyone
Never cried or missed
Never lied or dissed
That's how I know you're the one
My nine to five, my late nights and morning after
My skin to skin, lip to lip moans and laughter
I tried to man up and act like it wasn't that serious
Tried to convince myself I didn't need to settle down
And my affection for you was temporary
But on the contrary, time away from you made me
Miserable and forced me to keep it real
Truth is, there's never been a woman who could make me
Commit to what I feel
That's how I know this shit is real
Our connection
Our affection
We were always meant to be
I love you, Keva

N'Kyenge Ayanna

Prologue

We just finished round three and I am spent. Damarion takes my body to heights it's never been. Each time that we are together is better than the last. He's had me in positions that I had no idea my body could conform. The way he uses his tongue to bless every crevice of my honey pot has to be a sin. His dick is a work of art. It's the perfect length, the perfect width, and has the perfect curve. It fills me to the brim as if it was made specifically for me.

I've secretly lusted after Damarion for years. He and my twin brother, Kevan, have been best friends since we were in middle school. Back then we paid each other no mind. But I can tell you the first time that merely being in his presence caused my pussy to throb. I can remember the exact moment that he first took notice of the woman I had become. I could see it in his eyes. The way his gaze lingered. The way he licked his lips as if he could taste the fruit between my legs every time he laid eyes on me. The way he had to adjust his dick after being in my company for an extended amount of time.

Three months ago, we lost the battle we had been fighting against our feelings for each other. With that came three months of sneaking around. Three months of not being able to share the joy he makes me feel with the world. Three months of pretending like I'm not in love with him. Three months of my betrayal to another man.

"Where'd you go?" he asked. "Where's your head?"

He was lying between my legs with his head on my stomach after pulling an orgasm out of me with his mouth that had me in tears. The only sound that could be heard was the labored breaths that I released as I got lost in my thoughts and attempted to come down from my high.

"Just thinking," I replied.

"Don't do that. When you do that it puts you in a bad space. Let's enjoy our time."

"I can't help it. I can't keep doing this. I'm in a whole relationship with somebody else but I'd rather be with you," I complained. *"And let's not forget about your situation.*

"First of all, I told you not to bring that nigga up. I couldn't care less about his ass. Clearly whatever y'all got goin' on ain't shit or your pussy juice wouldn't be all over my face and my dick right now. And I don't have a situation. But Kevan...he ain't down with us being together. He told me straight up not to fuck with you and I promised him I wouldn't."

"I don't care about any of that."

"I know, baby, but I do. That's eighteen years of friendship and I gave him my word. This shit is complicated."

"He'll be upset but eventually, I think he will forgive us both. Are you willing to take that risk?"

When he didn't respond after several minutes, I moved my body from underneath him and went to my bathroom to shower. I'm tired of this shit. I understand that he doesn't want to risk eighteen years of friendship with my brother. But I'm starting to think there's something else...or someone else...that he doesn't want to risk losing.

Keva Jamison

I looked at the time on my phone and became annoyed. I should have left my office an hour ago, yet I'm here I am, still at work. I'm not in the mood to hang out but spending my Friday night looking at this proposed marketing budget was not in the plans either. With that in mind, I closed my laptop and shoved it in my work bag, slipped out of my pumps and into my boots before I grabbed my purse out of my desk drawer.

After standing from my chair, I took a nice long stretch and yawn before walking over to the coat rack to get my outerwear and bundling up. It's February and one of the coldest months of the year in Chicago. That's one of the main reasons that I don't want to go out. Well, that and because I know I'm going to see *him*…and he'll probably be with *her*.

Thinking about Damarion made my va-jay-jay thump. The things that man did to my body should be illegal. It's one thing to have a big dick. I've had my share of well-endowed men in the past and it was such a disappointment when they didn't know what to do with it. A waste of damn dick. But not Damarion. *Shit!* He knew how to work that monster between his legs and I've been going through withdrawals ever since we ended our secret love affair.

Damn it! Now my panties are wet and I'm horny. It's not like I can't have sex. I do have Tyson…for now anyway. When he comes back from his business trip, I *have* to break up with him. I can't pretend anymore, even if I wanted to. Although it's not the reason I'm breaking up with him, he fits in the category of big dick, big waste. None of that even matters because Damarion took ownership of my pussy and hasn't given it back. *I hate him.* Who am I fooling? *I love him.* But that's neither here nor there.

As soon as I walked out of the building the cold air took my breath away. With my mace in hand, I hurried down the block to the parking garage where my car was parked. I entered and made my way to my car on the third floor. Once inside, I locked the doors and pushed the start button.

As soon as my Bluetooth connected, my phone rang. I looked at the dashboard and saw it was my best friend, Farrah. We were paired as roommates our freshman year of college at Southern Illinois University at Carbondale and were inseparable from that point on. She's going to kill me when she finds out all the shit I've been keeping from her. Although she is my best friend, I can't risk telling her what's been going on just in case she decides to pillow talk with my twin brother, who is her fiancé.

"I'll be there in an hour," I said as soon as I picked up.

"An hour! What the hell Keva?" she yelled into the phone.

"I know, I know. I was finishing up something at work and lost track of time. I already know what I'm wearing. I just need to take a quick shower."

"Ugh! You make me sick! We'll be there in twenty minutes. Now we have to wait to eat and I'm hungry as hell," she complained.

"Shut your greedy ass up. Are you sure you don't have a little Kevan baking?" I joked.

"Hell-the-fuck-naw! Don't jinx me like that either!"

"I don't know why you act like having my baby would be so bad, Farrah." That came from my brother, Kevan, who

I'm sure is driving. He and Farrah have been together for almost two years and engaged for six months.

"Not until you change my last name. Dammit, Keva! Look what you done started. I'll see you in an hour. Hurry up!" With that, she ended the call.

Kevan started begging her for babies a few months into the relationship and she keeps telling him the same thing. Farrah refuses to pop out any babies for any man that is not her husband, no matter how much he claims to love her. He thinks that because they are engaged and have a wedding date set that it doesn't matter but Farrah ain't falling for it.

Kevan and Farrah are definitely relationship goals. When they met, it was a true definition of love at first sight...at least for him. He has never been one to play around with a girl's heart and for as long as I can remember, he's talked about finding his wife. Let him tell it, as soon as he laid eyes on Farrah he knew that she was it for him.

I give credit to my parents because they gave us the blueprint and have been a great example of Black Love. They met right after they graduated from graduate school and it was a whirlwind romance. They were married less than six months after they started dating and have been married for thirty years. It's been amazing watching their love and now, with no children in the house and them being retired, they still love on each other like they are newlyweds. I can't wait to fall in love with a man that isn't afraid to love me back, get married, and start my own legacy of Black Love.

An hour and a half later, I pulled up in front of the restaurant/lounge and handed my keys over to the valet. I walked in and looked around for my brother and best friend but didn't see them anywhere.

"Hi! Do you have a Jamison on your list?" I asked the hostess.

She looked at her clipboard before saying, "Oh, yes! Follow me!"

I followed her to the back area of the restaurant/lounge until we came to a private room with closed doors. She stopped in front of the doors and turned to me.

"Your party is inside. Enjoy your evening."

She walked away and I stood there for a moment trying to figure out why Kevan would rent a party room for tonight. Deciding that the only way to find out was to go inside, I shrugged out of my coat and hung it on the coat rack just outside of the room then gripped the door handle and pulled it open.

"Surprise!" everyone screamed, scaring the shit out of me.

"What the heck is going on?" I said to myself as I looked around the room.

There were faces of a few family members and friends that I don't see very often, some I hadn't seen in years. My eyes scanned the room for Kevan and Farrah but they were nowhere to be found. Suddenly, I felt some arms wrap around me from behind.

"Surprise, baby!" Tyson kissed my neck and I turned around.

"Tyson? What are you doing here? What is this?" I asked in confusion.

He had been out of town for the past week for his job. He's a software engineer for a company that has offices in several states and a few international locations. He travels a lot and I wasn't expecting him back until tomorrow. As confused and slightly annoyed as I was, I took in his handsome face. He's what us Black folks would call a pretty boy. Standing about six-two, lean body, light-skinned, soft curly hair, hazel eyes.

"I wanted to surprise you," he said.

Looking behind me, he signaled who I would assume was the DJ and the music lowered. I turned around when the DJ's voice came over the mic.

"Wassup everyone! Y'all having a good time?" he boomed. The crowd hooted and hollered.

"That's wassup! The guest of honor has arrived. Turn your attention to that beautiful couple near the entrance."

I turned to the entrance to look for the couple that the DJ was referring to and Tyson was on his knees.

"What are you doing down there?" I grabbed his arm and tried to pull him to his feet with no success.

The crowd became oddly quiet and someone with a cordless mic appeared and put it up to Tyson's mouth.

What the hell is going on here?

"Keva, I know this may sound cliché. After our first date, I knew that I wanted to make you my wife. You are everything that I could ever want in the woman that I'm spending my life with. Our connection is deeper than anyone could ever understand. It's not just physical, but mental and spiritual as well. Keva, would you do me the honor of being my wife?"

He opened the box and a beautiful princess cut diamond ring blinded me. I looked at him, speechless and in disbelief.

Wait! What? Did he just propose to me? This is a surprise all right. Is he serious?

Listening to his proposal, I couldn't help but wonder if he and I are in the same relationship. While he feels like we have a deep connection, I don't feel like we connect at all. On paper, he's the perfect guy. He has a great job, great income, nice to look at, and he treats me well. I do care about him but that connection he spoke of is nonexistent for me.

"Uhh...marry you...I...uhh, Tyson, you want to marry me?"

He remained on his knees waiting for the answer that I didn't want to give. I can't embarrass him in front of all these people? He doesn't deserve that.

I looked around the room and everyone looked on, anticipating me accepting his proposal. My head began to spin, my mouth was dry, my armpits were beginning to sweat, and tears ran down my face.

"Tyson," I began.

My words were interrupted as the party room doors opened abruptly and sent chills through my body. I don't know if that chill was because of the temperature or because of who walked in.

My eyes connected with the man that I was in love with that was too afraid to love me back. His loyalty to someone else, while admirable, wouldn't allow him to give himself to me. I could see the moment he realized what was going on. His eyes flickered with pain and confusion but he made no attempts to interfere. If he said the word, I would break Tyson's heart without a second thought.

"Keva," Tyson's voice drew my attention back to him. "Will you marry me?" he asked again with a hopeful look in his eyes, not knowing that the man I want to marry is standing behind him.

"Tyson, I," was all I could bring myself to say…until I saw her.

Seemingly out of nowhere, she appeared and looped her arm through his. My eyes met his again and I could swear they were willing me to say no. But he didn't step up, he didn't stop me, he didn't rescue me, so I did what needed to be done.

"Yes, Tyson, of course, I will marry you!" I finally accepted his proposal.

The crowd went crazy as Tyson slid the ring on my finger. He got on his feet and wrapped his arms around me in a loving embrace.

"Thank you, baby. You just made me the happiest man on earth." He kissed me gently on my lips and then my forehead.

Very conveniently, Kevan and Farrah appeared, along with my parents and Tyson's parents. My mom was the first to say something. I'm sure that she is over the moon about this. She thinks that Tyson is perfect for me, has practically planned our wedding, and is always talking about the beautiful hazel-eyed grandbabies we gon' give her. As our immediate family dished out hugs and congratulatory remarks, I willed myself to wake up from this nightmare.

Farrah tried to sneak away from me but I latched onto her arm and walked her to a corner. The look on her face let me know that she knew I was pissed.

"Farrah! Why didn't you warn me?" I whispered although it was unnecessary because of the noise level in the room.

"I didn't know until we got here and Kevan took my phone because he thought I might ruin the surprise. No one told me because they thought I'd tell you."

"I can't believe this shit! You know how I feel about Tyson. I mean, he's a good guy...a great guy actually. I just...I just don't---," I couldn't even find the right words to express how I felt about Tyson.

"You don't love him. It's plain and simple. You care for him but you don't love him. Why'd you say yes then, Keva?"

"I...I guess I didn't want to embarrass him. I don't know. Maybe it won't be that bad being married to him."

"Keva, you can't marry that man. I don't know what else to tell you except you can't marry him."

With that, Farrah hugged me and went back to join the party. Once they saw that I was alone, a few more people approached me to give their congratulations. I was gracious and kept a fake smile on my face but on the inside, I knew this wasn't right. A few hours ago, I was planning how I was going to break up with him and now we are engaged. This is so wrong and I feel horrible. As soon as I had a free moment, I snuck off to the bathroom to collect my thoughts.

I was thankful that no one was in the bathroom. I looked at my reflection in the mirror as I adjusted the brown fitted sweater dress that I was wearing. I don't even recognize the person in the mirror. The old me would have never accepted a proposal from someone she didn't love. She would have ended this relationship when she realized that her feelings for him would never go beyond platonic.

"Why is this my life?"

Avoiding Damarion had become my only goal since we went our separate ways. Seeing him was too hard. It forced me to accept that he didn't want to commit to me. I've only seen him a couple of times in the last two months when he popped up at my parent's house while I was there. The last night that we were together things were left in limbo. When I got out of the shower he was gone and made no efforts to initiate contact with me in the days and weeks that followed. That pretty much confirmed that we were done and that shit hurt.

Damarion was everything. With him I experienced fireworks, rumbling in the pit of my stomach, and the thought of being around him sends my libido to another planet.

Tyson and Damarion couldn't be more different in the looks department, although both are fine. Damarion has a bit more ruggedness to his look. He's a couple of inches taller than Tyson, with chocolate colored skin, a low Caesar cut with waves, dark brown almond-shaped eyes that penetrate my soul every time he looks at me. Oh, and his lips…perfectly kissable, encased in the beard that he grew out in the winter months.

"Whew!" I fanned myself trying to cool down and decided that a splash of cool water on my face may be just what I needed.

Damarion Sanders

I knew Keva had a nigga. They've been together for a good minute, almost a year, I think. Those three months we spent together, Keva was mine. I don't care what she had going on with that nigga. Her mind, soul, and body belonged to me. Hell, they still do as far as I'm concerned.

I've been kickin' it with this woman named Trinity for about six months but I've made it clear to her that we are not in a relationship. We aren't exclusive but I'm sure that's what she wants. Keva is the only woman that I've ever considered being exclusive with.

This situation is not an easy one. Kevan and I have been best friends for eighteen years. My history with women is not the greatest and he's seen me run through too many to count. I can admit that when I first started checking for Keva I wasn't ready to settle down. When Kevan noticed how I was looking at her he straight up told me that if I fucked with his sister and broke her heart, he would fuck me up and our friendship was done. I promised him I wouldn't. If I had acted on my feelings then I'm sure it wouldn't have ended well. But that was years ago and my whole mentality has changed since then. I'm thirty years old now and I'm not on the same bullshit I was five years ago.

Although we are best friends, more like brothers, Kevan and I are polar opposites when it comes to relationships. He's always preferred relationships over sleeping around. Not to say he hasn't had a one night stand here and there over the years. It wasn't something he did often. He would always say, "I'm looking for my wife."

I, on the other hand, have never had the desire to be in a relationship. I didn't even attempt to get to know a woman well enough to find out if she was relationship material. I got what I wanted a few times and dipped. My parents have been hounding me for the past few years to settle down. My mom, especially, doesn't understand why I can't find a nice girl to bring home, marry and give her some grandbabies. My pops though, I think he understands.

I remember him telling me, when I was about fourteen or fifteen, that he and my mom shouldn't have married so young. My parents were high school sweethearts. When it came time for them to graduate, he didn't have a plan and didn't want to go to college. My mom had gotten accepted to Howard University and was excited about it. He felt that he might lose her and began to panic then came to the conclusion that he should propose.

He did and they got married before she went off to school and he joined the Navy. The early years of their marriage was a struggle. They were young and didn't know the first thing about being married and they were doing it long distance. He physically cheated, she emotionally cheated, and they almost ended up divorced before they had a chance to live as a married couple. My mother is a retired elementary school teacher and my father retired from the Navy and is now a minister and they've been married for thirty-eight years. Obviously, they worked it out, however, knowing all of that is why I was in no rush to settle down...until Keva.

Five months ago, a group of us were hanging out and I ended up taking Keva home. It was extremely foggy and she convinced me to stay at her place that night instead of driving home. It didn't take much convincing but I didn't plan to act on the feelings I had for her. We ended up sleeping together and after that first time, we couldn't stay away from each other. It went on for three months and at no point did I have the desire to be with anyone else. Explain to me how I've never had the desire to be faithful to one woman and when I do, she belongs to someone else. *Ain't that some Karma for you?*

It's been two months since the last time we were together. Keva and her good ass pussy got Trinity thinking a nigga need Viagra or some shit 'cause my mans won't stay hard for her. I honestly don't know what's keeping her around. For me, she's convenient.

When I walked into that party room and saw that nigga on his knees, proposing to my girl, it took everything in me to keep from acting a complete fool. I couldn't take my eyes off Keva and I knew that she felt my gaze penetrating her soul when my eyes connected with hers. She's wearing her hair straight and it's flowing past her shoulders. Her chocolate skin is glowing, more than usual. Her dimples are on display and she's not even smiling. She can pretend like my presence isn't doing something to her but I know different.

I stood, frozen, as I waited for her to refuse his proposal. I know she's not crazy enough to accept it. But she proved me wrong. She has lost her fuckin' mind. When I heard her say those words, 'Yes, Tyson, of course, I will marry you', I yanked my arm out of Trinity's grasp and barge out of the room. Trinity's followed me and asked me what was wrong.

"Nothing but I need you to go home."

"But we just got here," she whined.

"I know but I realized that there's something I forgot to take care of. I'm leaving out shortly and I won't have time to take you home."

I don't know if she believed that lie but she didn't put up too much more of a fight, thank God. Maybe the promise

I made to her telling her to wait up for me helped. I gave her some money for an Uber and she left without further protest.

I turned to go back inside and I saw Keva going to the bathroom. When I opened the door to the women's bathroom, Keva was bent over the sink splashing her face with water. I watched her as she finished, grabbed the paper towels that she had placed on the sink and dabbed her face a few times. When she opened her eyes, I could see her body jump in surprise when she saw me behind her in the mirror.

"Shit, Damarion! What the hell?" She turned around to face me and leaned against the sink.

I looked her up and down, taking in her beauty. The dress she had on enhanced her already shapely body. But there was something different about her. She looked a little thicker and her face was a bit fuller.

"How you been?"

She folded her arms across her chest and put all of her weight on one leg, sticking out her hip.

"You're here with Trinity, worry about her." She threw the paper towels in the garbage and tried to walk around me but I locked the door and stood in front of it.

"I'd rather be with you. I miss you."

"You're with who you want to be with or you wouldn't be with her."

"Do you want to marry him, Ke?"

She looked at me and then looked away but didn't answer.

"Ke, I need to know. Do I still have a chance?"

Instead of answering she tried to move me away from the door but it was pointless. I put my hand against her chest and backed her against the wall. I leaned in so close that the tips of our noses were touching and I could feel her breath on my lips. I squeezed her thigh then pushed my hand underneath her dress, brushing two fingers against her pussy. My lips grazed hers and traveled to her neck. I love her scent and I've been missing it like crazy.

"This still my pussy, Ke?" I mumbled into her neck.

When she didn't answer, I moved the crotch of her panties to the side and pushed those same two fingers into her soaking wet center.

"Hmm," she moaned as she grinded against my fingers.

I worked my fingers in and out, using my thumb to massage her g-spot in a circular motion. Her breathing picked up letting me know that her release was on the way.

"Hmmm," she moaned again. "D, please."

After sucking on her neck hard and long enough to leave my mark, I kissed and licked the same spot to sooth the pleasurable pain. She loved that shit.

"Dammit!" she whispered as she came and her juices flowed onto my fingers.

I lifted my head and looked in her eyes as I pulled my fingers out of her juicy box. Bringing them to my mouth, I licked her sweet nectar from one of my fingers until I was satisfied, then put the other finger between her lips, forcing her to taste herself.

"Naw," I said as she enjoyed her flavor. "That nigga ain't hittin' it right. You came too quick. This pussy still mine."

Then I put my hand back underneath her dress and ripped off her panties. She gasped in shock.

"We need to talk. I don't know what the fuck you thought you had planned with that nigga and I don't care. Cancel that shit. Matter of fact, cancel him. You can't marry him. I won't let you!"

"You can't---,"

"You heard what the fuck I said, Ke!" he interrupted.

I put her panties up to my nose and inhaled deeply before stuffing them in my pocket, unlocking the door and leaving her there with no panties and a wet ass. I thought about going to the men's room to wash my hands but I'm a nasty nigga and I don't want to wash Keva's scent away.

Leaving the bathroom, I went outside to clear my head. Keva's words accepting Tyson's proposal were on repeat in my head. I know she doesn't love him. I know she doesn't want to marry him. Her heart belongs to me. But she accepted his proposal. *Why did she accept his proposal? Has her feelings changed?*

Keva

After not seeing Tyson for a week and us getting engaged tonight, he wasn't happy when I turned down his invitation to come to his place and I didn't invite him to mine. I'm sure he wanted to 'celebrate' but the thought of having sex with him right now didn't sit well with me. I ended up lying to him saying that I didn't feel good and I had to go in early to work tomorrow, promising him that we could spend the afternoon and evening together when I was done. That seemed to pacify him, thank goodness. Most men would have put up more of a fight but not Tyson. He rarely puts up a fight about anything to be honest.

When I pulled into my spot in the parking garage of my condo, I saw Damarion's car parked in my visitor's space. I took a deep breath and asked God to give me the strength to resist him. After a few moments, I reached for the door handle but Damarion opened it before I could.

"Why are you here? Tyson could have been with me!" I gave him all the attitude that I could muster up as I stepped out of my car and stood in front of him.

"You knew I wasn't playin' with your ass."

"The way you played with my heart for three months, what else would I expect! Ain't nothin' here for you, Damarion. Tyson and I are engaged now. I won't keep betraying him." I yelled, knowing that this would be the world's shortest engagement but Damarion didn't need to know that. I turned around to walk away and he slammed my car door.

"Keva!" he yelled.

Something about his tone caused me to stop in my tracks. He sounded…desperate. I turned around to face him and the look of despair that he wore weakened me. The strength I prayed for was nowhere to be found.

He took two steps toward me and grabbed the back of my neck. Bringing my face to his, he rested his forehead against mine and pecked my lips once, then again, then again, before his mouth consumed mine in a passionate kiss.

I wanted to push him away. I promised myself that I wouldn't get caught up in his web until he was ready to commit…until he chose my heart. But the moment our lips connected, all I wanted to do was be tangled in his web.

We kissed as if it were the only thing keeping us alive. Somehow, my back ended up against the back of my car with Damarion pushing up against me. I could feel his erection pressing against my stomach.

"Ke, baby, I missed you," he said against my lips.

His hands cuffed my ass cheeks and he lifted me onto the trunk. Before I could refuse him, my legs were on his shoulders and he dove his head into my pussy. There was no chance I was going to deny myself this pleasure.

"D, oh my God!" My screams echoed in the parking garage.

Damarion French kissed my pussy like he was the one who invented the act. His tongue dipped in, out, and around like he was searching for a buried treasure. I tried to refrain from screaming out in ecstasy but it was pointless.

"Shit! D, baby, I'm about to cum! Fuck!" I screamed.

The more verbal I was the harder he went. Today was no exception. Damarion has this thing that he does that sends me over the edge. He waits until I'm on the verge of erupting, stiffens his tongue and pushes it deep inside my hole. Then he presses his nose against my g-spot and hums.

"Oh damn!" My orgasm hit me and I almost climbed backwards up the back window but Damarion was holding my thighs so tight that running was out of the question.

When he released my clit from hostage, I opened my eyes to see the ceiling of the garage. Taking a moment to catch my breath and process my thoughts, I realized that my bare ass was on my car, I still had on my coat, and my purse was still on my shoulder. However, none of that shit meant anything to Damarion and I was too weak to put up a fight.

He moved my legs from his shoulders to his waist and lifted me from the trunk. I pulled my dress down as much as I could and wrapped my arms around his neck while locking my ankles behind him. He carried me as if I weighed nothing through the garage and into the building. My eyes were closed but I felt him fumbling for his keys which let me know that we were at my condo.

Kay Shanee

Damarion

As soon as we were inside her condo, it was on. We left a trail of clothes leading to her living room and that's as far as we made it. Keva reached behind her and unhooked her bra, releasing her full c-cup breasts, making my mouth water. When she reached down to unzip one of her boots I had to stop her.

"Leave 'em!" I demanded. "Turn around...put your hands on the couch...bend over."

I stroked my dick as she followed each instruction. I knew she was ready for this dick but the need to taste her again overwhelmed me. I turned around, got on my knees, and buried my face in her mound.

"Ahhh," she moaned as she almost lost her balance.

Both of my hands were planted on her ass, pressing her into my face while I devoured her pussy. Her legs began to tremble, letting me know that she was close to exploding. But I wasn't ready for her to release yet.

"Dammit, D!" she complained when she no longer felt my mouth connected to her pussy.

Before she could get too upset, I pushed my dick into her wet walls. The sound she made upon my entrance and the way her walls gripped my dick had me ready to bust. I know it's been a minute but she felt more amazing than ever before.

"Whose pussy is this, Ke?" I asked as I pounded her from the back.

Her stubborn ass didn't answer but that's cool. I reached around with one hand to stimulate her g-spot with two fingers and used the other hand to play with her nipples while I dug deep inside of her.

"Answer me, Ke. Whose pussy is this?" I whispered before taking her earlobe in my mouth.

"Hmm, shit!" was all she said.

"This ain't my pussy no more?" I pushed down on her back, creating the perfect arch, then grabbed both hips and slammed into her juicy box.

"Ahh, fuck yes, D. It's yours! I'm about to cum."

Her walls tightened around my dick, milking my seeds into her sweet haven. I pray she's still on the pill because pulling out was not an option.

"Damn, Ke!" I fell forward against her back as we both caught our breath.

"You got what you wanted, Damarion. You can leave now." I could hear the sadness in her voice.

I slowly pulled out of her and took a few steps back, allowing her room to move.

"What the fuck is that supposed to mean, Ke? You act like this is all it is with us!" I yelled.

"Isn't it? This is all we can do." She punched me in the chest and stomped to her bedroom.

"Keva, baby, this ain't what I want either." I went after her, dick swinging and all. "I want you, baby! I want to be with you."

She stopped at her bedroom door and turned to look at me. We were an arm's length apart and I wanted to reach out and pull her to me but I refrained.

"These past two months fucked me up. I missed the hell outta you. You can't marry him, Ke, please."

"Would you be here if he hadn't proposed?"

I didn't answer right away because I took a minute to think about it.

"I can't honestly say."

Tears welled up in her eyes and it broke my heart that I was the cause of them.

"I love you, Ke. Maybe it took him proposing to you for me to see that. But I love the hell outta you and the only way you marrying that nigga is over my dead body."

"You…you love me?"

"I do…and I'm sorry it took me as long as it did to confess to you what I've felt on my heart for a long time. I'll find a way to tell Kevan. I know I gotta come to him correct. He's like a brother to me and it would be fucked up if me loving you ended our brotherhood. But us being apart can't happen. Now you need to call off this engagement. Take that fuckin' ring off and give that shit back. You're mine!"

"Tell me again."

"Tell you what?"

"That you love me."

"I love you.

Keva

Those three words were like music to my ears. In all of our moments of passion, they were never exchanged. I've loved him for a long time. I fell in love with Damarion the moment our lips first met the first time we kissed. I never verbally expressed my feelings because, although I could feel it, I was afraid that the sentiment would not be returned if I said it first.

"I love you, too," I finally expressed.

His lips landed on mine and he moved me backward until we fell on my bed. My legs automatically went around his waist. As we grinded against each other the friction created heat between my legs. As his dick began to play peek-a-boo with the entrance to my sacred spot, I was overcome with a wave of nausea.

"Ugh!" I groaned pushing him away.

He moved to the side and I shot off the bed and ran to my bathroom. I made it to the toilet just in the nick of time to vomit up the little bit of food I was able to eat tonight. Every time I thought it was over another wave hit me. Damarion was gracious enough to put my hair up and rub my forehead with a cool towel.

"You good?" he asked as he helped me off the floor.

"Yeah, I think so." I grabbed my toothbrush and proceeded to brush my teeth.

When I walked back into my bedroom, I noticed that Damarion had put on his boxers. I grabbed my robe, putting it on and finally taking my boots off before sitting next to him on the bed.

"Is there something you need to tell me, Ke?" he asked with a look of concern.

I looked at my hands and he lifted my chin forcing me to look him in the eyes.

"Umm, for the last few weeks I haven't been feeling the best. I went to the doctor on Monday and uhh, yeah, I'm pregnant."

"Pre...pregnant. How did you...I thought you were on the pill."

"I am...well, I was until Monday. But remember when I had that sinus infection and I was on antibiotics?" He nodded. "Yeah, well, I forgot they weaken birth control pills."

"Are you sure it's mi---," I gave him a look daring him to finish asking that question.

"Don't!"

"Keva, I think it's a fair question."

"I've never fucked him, or anybody else for that matter, without a rubber, D. Never! I'm almost three months. He was out of the country for work for three weeks. It's yours, D."

"You don't even look pregnant. Your stomach is flat. Are you sure you're that far along?"

I got up and went to my top drawer and pulled out the ultrasound that I and tucked in there for safekeeping. I sat back on the bed and gave it to him.

"Look at the top. It says I'm eleven weeks, two days."

"Shit! You been fuckin' that nigga with my seed inside of you?"

"I mean, yeah, a few times. I didn't know I was pregnant until five days ago, Damarion. He's been traveling a lot so it's only been a few times," I explained.

30

"That's fucked up though. You carryin' my seed and fuckin'---,"

"What the fuck did you expect? He's my boyfriend!" I yelled and pushed away from him, attempting to get off the bed but he pulled me back down.

"He's not your fuckin' boyfriend. I'm yo nigga, period. I'm sorry, okay. I don't like to think about you being with him like that but...let's not talk about his ass no more."

"Okay. Are you happy about the baby?" I asked as tears gathered in my eyes.

"I am happy. I wouldn't want anyone else in this world to have my baby. I'm just in shock." He pulled me into his arms and kissed the top of my head. "Are you happy?"

I didn't say anything but nodded my head.

"Why didn't you tell me right away?" he pulled me back to look at me.

I shrugged my shoulders before answering. "I wasn't going to keep it from you. I needed some time to wrap my head around the idea of being a single mother, disappointing my parents and my brother...and then there's Tyson."

"Fuck that nigga. And there was no way I was gon' let you raise our baby alone. What kinda fuck nigga do you think I am?"

"The kind that doesn't want to commit to me and using his friendship with my brother as a crutch."

"Damn, that's how you feel?" I nodded. "I know it took me a minute to come around. You gotta understand that the feelings I have for you, I've never experienced them before. I was in denial but there is no question that what I have with you, and now our baby, is worth it. If Kevan can't accept that I'm in love with you then it is what it is."

I never wanted it to come down to Damarion having to choose a relationship with me over his friendship with my brother. But it feels good that he is finally willing to do that.

I kissed him and allowed my lips to linger for several seconds. "I'm exhausted. Can we go to bed now?"

We both stood and he pulled the covers back allowing me to get in first. I took off my robe and tossed it on the floor before scooting to the other side and he got in next to me. I put my back to his chest and he pulled me close, nuzzling my neck with his nose.

"I love you, Ke."

"I love you, D."

******

What seemed like only a few hours later, I heard my phone blaring in the other room. I ignored it but the caller was persistent as hell.

"What Kevan? Why are you calling me like somebody died?" I yelled when I answered.

"I'm outside your condo and I can't remember the code. Let me in!"

"Wait! What? Why are you here?" I said as I began to panic.

"Just buzz me in," he persisted.

Shit! This is bad. This is all bad.

"Keva, let me up!" he yelled into the phone.

"Okay, okay!" I hung up the phone and ran through my condo like a mad woman picking up Damarion's and my clothes from last night and tossing them into my room.

"Oh shit! Damarion!" I ran back to my room and pushed him on the shoulder.

"Baby, baby, wake up!"

"Huh? Wassup?" he replied without opening his eyes.

"Kevan is here! I don't want him to find out about us like this. Don't leave this room, okay."

"Okay," he said, again without opening his eyes.

"D, did you hear me?" I shook him.

"Yeah, baby. I won't come out." Seconds later he was asleep again. I don't know if he heard me or not but I pray he did.

My phone rang again and I looked at the screen to see it was Kevan calling again. *Shit!* I left my room, closing the door tightly behind me and hustled over to my front door to buzz Kevan in.

He barged right in without knocking. "Damn, Sis. What took you so long to let me in?"

"I was sleep, nigga. Don't come over here unannounced talking shit. Now, what do you want?"

He sat on the couch, right where Damarion had me bent over last night, and put his feet on my coffee table.

"Kev, if you don't get your damn feet off my table!" I tightened my robe before walking over and knocking his feet off my table. "Now why are you here?"

"I wanted to check on you. How you feelin' about the engagement? I mean, I'm not a woman but your reaction was not what I thought it'd be, Sis."

"I'm good. I just wasn't expecting that. We've never discussed marriage so I think I was in shock," I replied without looking him in his eyes.

He looked at me trying to gauge whether or not I was telling the truth. I've never been able to lie to Kevan. He knew me almost better than I knew myself.

"You don't want to marry him, do you? You know you can't lie to me, Ke."

"I'm not---," I started to lie.

"Baby, have you seen my phone?" I heard my bedroom door open and turned around to see Damarion walking out in his boxers rubbing his eyes. I wanted to crawl under my couch.

"What the fuck?" Kevan jumped up and charged Damarion.

Damarion was still half asleep and didn't even see Kevan coming. He fell on the floor with Kevan on top of him.

"Nigga I told you to stay the fuck away from her," Kevan yelled and swung but Damarion blocked the punch to his face.

"Kevan stop!" I screamed as I tried to pull him off Damarion to no avail.

"She ain't one of yo hoes! This my fuckin' sister!"

Damarion finally got his bearings together and was able to push Kevan off of him. They were on their feet but I could tell that he didn't want to fight Kevan but he wasn't gon' lay there and get his ass beat. Kevan was swinging and Damarion was ducking and dodging. If this were anyone else it would be quite comical.

"Kevan! Please, stop. It's not like that," I tried again to explain. Somehow I was able to get between them putting Damarion behind me and Kevan in front of me.

"Kevan! It's not what you think. We're in love!" I told him.

"Man, that's bullshit. Not the way this nigga runs through bitches! I told you not to fuck with my sister, D."

"Man, Kev. This ain't what you think, bruh. I get why you feel that way but I'm not even that nigga no more. She's it for me," Damarion told him.

"You expect me to believe you and you was just with a bitch last night?"

Kevan shook his head and directed his next statement to me.

"You know what? I don't know why I give a fuck. Obviously, I don't know as much about you as I thought I did. You fuckin' two niggas at the same time. That's some hoe shit right there, Sis." *Damn, that hurt!*

"Nigga---," Damarion started and moved towards Kevan before I stopped him.

"Don't!" I put my hand against his chest. "He's just telling me how he feels. You can leave now, Kevan."

He turned to get his phone from the couch and left without saying another word.

As soon as the door closed behind Kevan, I broke down.

Damarion

"**B**aby, I'm sorry." I pulled Keva into a hug.
"I told you to stay in my room. I didn't want him to find out like this," she cried.

"I know, baby. I was half asleep and I don't even remember you coming in there."

"Why does us being together upset him so much?" she asked.

We walked over to sit on the couch and I pulled her onto my lap.

"Kevan knows damn near everything about me and all he's ever seen is me run through women like crazy. He doesn't want me to hurt you."

"You won't, will you?"

"I would never hurt you intentionally, baby." I lifted her chin and kissed her lips. "Kevan will come around. He loves you and needs to see that I love you, too."

"You gon' show him?"

"I'm gon' show him and you." We kissed again, this time allowing our tongues to intertwine.

My hands traveled up her thighs and underneath her robe. Turning her body on my lap, she straddled me. A moan escaped her lips as I brushed my fingers over her mound. Reaching between us, she pulled my rock hard dick out of my boxers, put the head at her entrance and sank down.

"Uhh," she exhaled once my full length disappeared inside of her.

I pushed her robe from her shoulders and palmed both of her breasts in my hands. Squeezing her nipples, I gave them both attention by swiping my tongue over each of them feverishly.

Keva began to grind her hips in a circular motion and I could feel her walls tightening. I released her breasts, moved my hands to her hips and fucked her from the bottom, slamming her down aggressively.

"Shit, D! I'm cummin'!" she screamed.

In her moment of ecstasy, she leaned back, putting her in the perfect position for me to dig deep in her guts.

"Damn, Ke! This pussy---shit!" I felt my dick jerk inside of her, releasing my seeds into her tunnel.

I pulled her close and wrapped my arms around her as she rested her head on my shoulders. We sat quietly as we came down from our high.

Her phone interrupted our blissful moment and she sat up and leaned back to grab it from the table. When she looked at the screen, she frowned, answering it on speaker.

"Hey, Tyson!"

"Hey, baby! Did I wake you?"

"Not really, what's up?"

"Well, I got some bad news. Some shit went down at one of our offices in Dallas and I gotta fly out later tonight. I'll be gone until Thursday or Friday. I want to see you before I leave," Tyson explained.

She looked at me for permission and I nodded my head.

"I hope it's nothing too serious."

"Naw, it's not too serious but my boss wants me to handle it. I'll try to wrap this up quickly and be back by Valentine's Day on Thursday. Do you want me to stop by or do you want to meet somewhere?"

"Umm, you can come here. What time were you thinking?"

"Is two cool?"

"Yeah, that's fine," she agreed after looking at the time on her phone. "I'll see you then."

"Cool. Love you!"

If she returned the sentiment I was gon' toss her ass across this room.

"Okay. Talktoyoulaterbye!" she rushed that last part and ended the call.

"Do you love him, Ke?" I sat on the couch next to her.

She looked to be thinking about it before she answered which made me feel a way. "I care about him. I have love *for* him. But no, I don't *love him* love him," she answered with confidence. "Not like I love you." That made me smile.

"Have you ever told him you love him?"

She scrunched up her nose. "Umm, no. I don't throw those words around unless I mean them. He told me that I didn't have to say it, he could feel my love for him."

"Whack ass nigga! Why'd you even agree to marry his ass?"

She laid her head on my shoulder before answering.

"Because you didn't stop me."

Shit! I wanted to stop her.

She sat up before continuing. "Why didn't you stop me?"

"I didn't then but I am now. I'm just glad you willing to give me a chance to make it right, baby." I kissed her temple and rubbed her back.

"You need to end that shit with Trinity."

"I'm not in a relationship with her."

"She definitely thinks she's in a relationship with you."

"That's what she gets for thinkin'. I've never told that woman she was my girl."

"Yeah, whatever," she mumbled and tried to get up.

"Where you goin'?" I held her down by her hips ensuring that could feel my dick hardening inside of her. "I know you feel that."

"I'm gonna go shower then you can take me to out for breakfast."

"What if I want to stay in and have you for breakfast?" I took one of her nipples in my mouth.

"Then what am I gon' eat?" she spoke softly as she grinded her hips.

"I'll cook for you when I'm done feastin'!"

I picked her up in one swift move and laid her on the couch. She flung one of her feet over the back of the couch while the other foot rested on the floor, giving me ample access to my meal. Without further hesitation, I dove in. I can't seem to get enough of her.

Keva

Damarion refused to leave my condo. Tyson was set to arrive in about a half an hour and I'm running around trying to make sure that there is no evidence of Damarion in sight and he is refusing to leave.

"What do you think is gonna happen?" I asked him as he followed me throughout my condo.

"This is some heavy shit you're about to drop on him. You don't think things will get a little heated?"

"Tyson has never even raised his voice at me. I'm sure he'll be upset but I highly doubt he will do anything crazy," I reasoned.

I walked through the kitchen and living area one last time. Damarion fucked me all over the condo this morning which has me wiping everything down with Lysol and spraying everything with Febreze.

My sex life with Tyson pales in comparison to what I have with Damarion. I'm not dumb enough to believe that sexual chemistry can maintain a relationship but there needs to be something there. At least for me anyway.

"Keva, this man proposed to you last night. You accepted his proposal in front of all of your friends and family. You did that, knowing you were in love with

39

someone else and carrying someone else's seed. If I were him, I would want to choke the shit outta you."

I gasp and turned to look at him to see if he was serious.

"What? I'm serious," he confirmed as he pulled me into his arms.

"Fine, you can stay but promise me you will stay in the room this time."

He laughed. "Since I'm actually coherent and understand what you're asking, I can do that. I'll be on standby if that nigga gets outta pocket though."

"I'm sure he'll be fine. Hurt, but fine."

We stood like that, with his arms around my waist and mine around his neck, staring into each other's eyes for a moment.

"Why are you staring at me like that?"

He smiled before pressing his lips against mine. After a knee-weakening kiss, he pulled away and looked into my eyes again before speaking.

"No reason, baby. No reason, at all."

As if on cue, I heard my buzzer alerting me that someone was at my door.

"Oh shit, I need to put the ring back on." I ran to my room and grabbed it off my dresser. When I came out, Damarion was sitting on the arm of my couch wearing a scowl on his face.

Giving him a quick kiss, I gave him one last warning to stay in the room. He smirked before going to my room and closing the door. I looked around again, making sure nothing was out of place and buzzed him in.

After unlocking my door, I went to the kitchen to get myself a bottle of water. My stomach is doing cartwheels right now and I'm dreading this conversation. I jumped when I heard him knock on the door, even though I was expecting him.

"It's open!" I yelled from the kitchen.

Tyson walked in looking good enough to eat. I smiled as I approached him. He held his arms open for me and I gave him the hug that he was expecting.

"Hey, baby! Damn, I've been missing you." He hugged me tight and buried his face into my neck, leaving soft kisses. His hands travel to my ass and he squeezed and pressed me against his body.

"You getting thick, baby. I love it!" He leaned in for a kiss on the lips and I obliged. "You feeling any better?"

"I do. Let's sit down. I need to talk to you about something."

He took off his coat and flung it over one of the chairs in the kitchen. I grabbed his hand and pulled him to the coach. He sat down first and attempted to pull me to his lap but I maneuvered my way next to him.

"Am I in trouble? I know I've been traveling a lot lately but---,"

"No, Tyson. You're not in trouble. But what I have to say isn't good."

Lord help me get through this. I don't want to break his heart but I can't put his happiness above my own.

"What's up?"

"Promise to let me say what I need to say before you respond or react," I requested as I looked into those hazel eyes of his.

"Shit, Keva. What's goin' on?"

"Just promise me."

"Okay, I promise."

I took his hand in mine before continuing and took a deep breath.

"Yesterday, when you proposed, I shouldn't have accepted." I felt him tense up. "We have never talked about marriage, Tyson. I was completely caught off-guard. As much as I enjoy spending time with you, I don't feel the same way about you as you do about me. I thought that over time, my feelings would change. I care about you a lot and you're an amazing man but you're not the man for me."

There was a long, long silence. I couldn't stand to look him in his eyes anymore. Tears streamed down my face because it hurt me to do this but I had to follow my heart. I felt his hand on my chin, gently forcing him to face him.

"I knew that sometimes things felt forced. I just thought that eventually, you'd love me as much as I love you. We could be so good together, Keva. We could be everyone's relationship goals. We don't have to get married right away. A long engagement is fine with me."

"I can't, Tyson. I can't do that to you. I'm sorry but my heart belongs to someone else," I cried.

The look of devastation when he realized what I had said broke my heart.

"There's someone else?"

I couldn't answer verbally so I nodded instead.

"Who, Keva? Who does your heart belong to?"

"Tyson, that's not important."

"Yes, Keva. It is important. Have you been cheating on me?"

It felt as if his eyes were burning holes into my skin. I couldn't bear to look at him. He had long since let my hand go. Sitting up, he put his elbows on his knees and his head in his hand.

"Shit, Keva."

"I'm sorry, Tyson. I never meant for any of this to happen," I apologized again, knowing it would do no good.

"I need to go." He shot up off the couch but I grabbed his arm before he could go anywhere. He looked down at me with teary eyes.

"There's more."

"You haven't hurt me enough, Keva. What the fuck more could it be? You pregnant by the nigga?"

I let his arm go and looked away. I'm pretty sure that I'm going straight to hell. What kind of person does this to someone?

"Fuuuuccckkkkk!" he yelled and picked up the glass vase that was on my coffee table and threw it against the wall.

As I told Damarion, I've never heard Tyson raise his voice. I scooted my ass to the corner of the couch because I knew shit was about to be all bad. Damarion came his ass out of the room so quick and was in Tyson's face before all of the glass from the vase hit the floor.

"Aye, nigga. Calm yo ass down!" Damarion spat.

Tyson looked at Damarion like he was trying to process what he was seeing. He didn't move and he didn't say anything. He just stared at Damarion for an uncomfortably long time and then he looked at me.

"You know, when you introduced us, I didn't have a good feeling in my gut. I could never put my finger on it but anytime we were in the same space, I felt it."

"Tyson, I didn't mean for this to happen." I stood next to Damarion and slid the engagement ring off my finger. "You should take this back." I held it out for him to take it but he just looked at my hand.

"How do you know that baby isn't mine?"

"It's not." I grabbed his hand and placed the ring in his palm.

"I want a DNA test." He yanked his hand away from me with the ring in his palm.

"I'm twelve weeks. It happened when you were out of the country for three weeks. Tyson, we've never had unprotected sex. This isn't your baby."

"I want a test."

He angrily walked away, getting his coat from the kitchen before leaving. Damarion went and locked the door and sat next to me on the couch, where I had just collapsed. Pulling me onto his lap, I rested my head on his shoulder and cried.

"I ain't a heartless nigga…I'm gon' let you have a minute to mourn the end of whatever the fuck that was you had goin' on with that nigga. When that minute is up I better be the only nigga on your mind…and that's real talk, Ke."

Keva

This weekend went by in a blur. Parts of it have me on cloud nine and others have me feeling like shit. Monday came too quickly. I was still processing everything that occurred in that three-day span. I was tempted to take a few vacation days but decided against it since Damarion had to work and couldn't lay up with me.

I was immersed in the same proposed marketing budget that I intended to work on over the weekend but that never happened. There was a knock on my door, startling me a bit.

"Come in," I summoned.

My assistant, Heather, walked in with a cheesy smile on her face.

"What are you smiling about?" I asked.

"You have a delivery," she replied, still grinning.

"Okay." I stood and smoothed my skirt down before walking around my desk. "Where is it?"

I took a few steps towards my door but once I reached the threshold, I saw a huge bouquet of roses in front of me. I now had a cheesy smile on my face because I could tell that the person behind the flowers was Damarion.

Once he was completely inside my office, I dismissed Heather and she backed out and closed the door, still smiling like she knew a secret. I guess news of my engagement could have gotten back to someone here at the office through social media but I highly doubt it. No one would say anything to me about it unless I mentioned it to them anyway.

Damarion put the roses on my desk along with a Panera Bread bag that I hadn't noticed before then took off his coat. I watched him inquisitively, wondering what he was doing here. He looked so handsome in a pair of black dress pants and a fitted orange sweater that displayed his muscular upper body.

"Hey, Beauty," he said, pulling me against his body and wrapping his arms around my waist.

"Hey, what are you doing here?"

"I missed you…and I wanted to make sure you fed my baby."

"Aww, baby. You're so sweet." I kissed his lips then wiped off the remnants of my lipstick. "I didn't even realize it was anywhere near lunch time. Thank you!"

"No need to thank me. Just taking care of my girls," he stated confidently.

"Girls? What makes you think we're having a girl?" I asked as I moved the vase of roses to the bookshelf that I had in my office.

"I don't know. That's what my gut is tellin' me. Let's eat."

He took the food out of the bags and brought it over to the small table that I had in my office. I got two bottled waters out of the fridge and we sat next to each other on the couch.

"What did you get me?" I asked as he took the lid off of what looked to be a bowl of soup.

"Cream of chicken and rice soup and a half turkey bacon swiss sandwich." He handed me the soup then began to unwrap my sandwich.

"How do you know my favs?" I took the bowl from him and immediately ate a spoonful.

"Because we've ordered in from Panera damn near every time we've been together. I know how to pay attention and commit things to memory."

"Oh my God. I didn't realize how hungry I was," I ate another spoonful of soup almost before I had swallowed down the first.

We sat in a comfortable silence for a bit while we enjoyed our food. I was damn near inhaling my soup and Damarion looked at me with his eyes narrowed.

"You're eating for two so don't be skippin' meals and shit. I was doing some research and it said that you need to put something on your something every couple of hours. That'll help with your morning sickness, too."

He took a bite of his sandwich as I stared at him in disbelief.

"You've been doing some research? I guess you're gonna be one of those expectant fathers. I can see right now you're about to drive me crazy." I shook my head and continued eating my soup.

"Yup! Get ready." He leaned in for a kiss. "When do you want to tell our parents?"

"About us being together or about the baby?"

"Shit, both. May as well tell it all at the same time. You'll be showing soon, right?" he asked before taking the last bite of his sandwich then guzzling down half of the water bottle.

"Yeah, we should do it soon. I don't think Kevan will say anything but the sooner the better."

"How do you think your mom will handle you calling off the engagement? She seems like she likes that nigga."

"Who knows? She just wants grandbabies so she may not give a damn once I tell her I'm pregnant. Besides, we already know she loves you."

"Sounds like my mother. I can't tell you the last time I had a conversation with her where she didn't mention me settling down and giving her grandbabies."

"I guess it's good that we can make them both happy at the same time. This baby is going to be spoiled rotten."

We laughed as we stood and gathered up our garbage.

"You only took two bites of this sandwich, Ke," he pointed out.

"I know. I got full from the soup. I'll be hungry again before I leave and I can nibble on my sandwich." I took it from him, securing the wrapping and putting it in the fridge.

"You better stop bending over like that up in here. Making my dick hard and shit." He adjusted himself before pulling me into his arms.

"Your ass stay horny." I wrapped my arms around his neck while he squeezed my ass.

"Just for you, baby." His lips connected with mine and we got lost in a passionate kiss. When I moaned he pulled away.

"Nope. You tryin' to get me caught up with that moaning and shit. I gotta get back to work."

Damarion worked as a Human Resources Manager at a company in downtown Chicago. It actually wasn't too from here. We could probably have lunch together often.

"Thank you for lunch. That was sweet." I kissed him again.

"Anything for you. I'll see you tonight?" he phrased the last part as a question as if he was checking to see if the plan had changed.

"Naw, I got something to do," I replied with a serious face.

"The hell you gotta do?" His face frowned up and I couldn't stop myself from laughing.

"Damn, bae, I'm just playin'," I said through my laughter. "What time will you be over? I'll have dinner ready."

"Shit, if you cookin', as soon as I leave work. Now kiss me so I can go."

He squeezed my ass again while we kissed. "I love you."

"I love you, too."

I missed his presence as soon as he pulled away from me.

******

Not even an hour later, there was another knock on my door. It was slightly ajar so I summoned them in.

"Ms. Jamison, you have another visitor," Heather informed me, this time without the kool-aid smile on her face.

"Thank you! Send them in."

I sat back in my chair and waited for my visitor to enter my office. I was stunned when I saw who it was. She pranced on in, closed the door behind her and took a seat at the chair on the other side of my desk. Sitting back in the chair, she crossed her legs and we stared at each other briefly before I finally spoke.

"Trinity, how can I help you?"

"I knew something was going on between y'all but I didn't have proof. I could tell just by the way y'all looked at each other. I don't know how Tyson never saw it."

What she's saying is probably true but she's only been in my presence a handful of times and they were all *before* anything had ever happened between Damarion and I.

"I'm gonna ask you one more time, Trinity. How can I help you?

"You can help me by staying away from my man," she spat.

"What man is that, exactly?"

"You know who the fuck I'm talkin' about!" She sat up in her seat and pounded her fist on my desk while she yelled at me.

"First of all, bitch, lower your fuckin' voice. You will not come into my place of employment and act a fool because I will beat your ass," I whispered sternly through clenched teeth.

I didn't move from my relaxed position in my chair while I read her ass but she removed her hand from my desk and sat her ass back.

"Now, if you have a problem with something that your man is doing, you need to talk to him. I ain't got shit to do with that. Now get the fuck out!" I stood and walked around my desk to open the door.

"I'm pregnant." My steps halted.

"What did you say?" I looked at her, daring her to say that shit again, and she did.

"I'm pregnant…and I'm not raising this baby alone. You have a man…a fiancé…leave *my* man alone."

She got up and snatched the door open and walked out. I felt faint. She's lying. Damarion wouldn't do this to me. She has to be lying.

Damarion

L unch with Keva was just what I needed to get me through my day. The rest of the afternoon flew by and I couldn't wait to see her again. I stopped by my place when I left home to get some clothes for the next few days before heading over to her condo.

I called her to see if she needed me to pick up anything from the store on my way but her phone strangely went straight to voicemail. I called a few more times and it did the same thing. I didn't think too much into it until I punched the code in to get into the parking garage of her building. It didn't work. I called her again and just as it did before, it went straight to voicemail.

What the hell is goin' on here?

Not wanting to panic, I found a spot on the street to park and grabbed my overnight bag. I figured I could just go in through the main entrance. Fortunately, someone was going in when I arrived because I wasn't sure if the code would work.

Keva lived on the first floor and I had keys to her apartment. I damn near ran down the hallway, anxious to find out what was going on. I took my keys out when I got to the door. When I inserted them into the lock, I got the shock of my life...they didn't work. I looked at the number on the door to verify that I was at the right place. I was.

Instead of panicking, I knocked on the door lightly and called her name. "Keva, baby, what's going on? Open the door."

I put my ear up to the door and could hear nothing so I tried again. "Keva, I know you hear me knocking, open the door."

I waited for a response and got nothing. Right now, I'm confused as hell. Replaying the afternoon in my head, everything seemed fine. I don't know what could have happened when I left her office that would cause her to be ignoring me.

I began to worry that something may have happened to her so I went to the parking garage. I saw that her car was there and I approached it, looked inside, and touched the hood. Nothing looked out of place and the hood was still warm.

I went back inside and tried knocking again. I stayed there for half an hour before I gave up. I'm not even a hundred percent sure she's inside but I'm willing to bet she is.

When I got to my car, I didn't know where to go, or what to do. Mentally, I'm somewhere between worried and pissed off. I'm worried because something could have happened and I'm pissed off because she could also just be ignoring me. I decided to go to my parent's house to keep my mind off this situation.

I arrived about thirty minutes later and parked in the small driveway. I rang the doorbell and used my key to enter, called out for my parents right away.

"Ma, Pops, where y'all at?"

"I'm here in the kitchen and your father is downstairs in his cave," my mom called out.

I went to the kitchen and found my mom cooking dinner. Even though it's just her and my dad and I'm an only child, she still cooks most nights.

"Hey, Ma," I greeted, kissing her on the cheek and taking a seat at the kitchen table.

"Hey, Son. Dinner will be ready shortly. How was your day?"

I have dinner at my parent's house more times than not so my mom always makes enough for me.

"It was cool," I replied.

She turned to look at me. "What's wrong? You don't sound so good."

"Can I use your cell phone right quick, Ma? I'll only be a minute."

Her phone was on the table and I didn't wait for her to answer. I snatched it up and went upstairs to my old bedroom before she could ask any questions.

Finding Keva's number in the contacts, I pressed it and prayed she'd pick up.

"Hey, Auntie." I could hear the sadness in her voice although she was trying to hide it.

"Keva! What the fuck is going on?"

"Damarion?"

"You know who this is! Now answer my damn question!"

"Ask Trinity!" she yelled before she ended the call.

"Ask Trinity?" I repeated.

I ran back downstairs, two at a time, going back to the kitchen.

"Damarion, what's going on with you?" Ma questioned.

"I can't talk right now. Here's your phone. I gotta go." I kissed her cheek again and ran out of the door. I'm sure I'll have to explain later.

Once I started my car and it connected to Bluetooth, I called Trinity.

"Hey, Boo!" she answered.

"Trinity, I'm gon' ask you this one time. What the fuck did you tell Keva?"

"What are you talkin' about? I ain't tell that girl nothin' but the truth."

"Stop fuckin' playin' with me or I swear on my mama I'm gon' get my cousins to come fuck you up!"

She took an unnecessary dramatic ass deep breath before she said anything.

"I told her that I was pregnant."

"You did what? Are you fuckin' crazy?" I had to pull over because I was so pissed off I could have driven into a damn wall.

"I knew you were fuckin' around with her. I saw the way you looked at her, the way she looked at you. You'd have to be blind to not see that shit. She got a whole fiancé Damarion and I'm not givin' you up that easily. I knew if she thought I was pregnant she would leave you alone," she confessed.

"You lyin' ass bitch! You know damn well you not pregnant with my seed. I told you off top that I wasn't a relationship kinda nigga and you was cool with that. Now you're ass out here lyin' on my seeds. You better watch your back with your lyin' ass!"

I ended the call, still fuming. I can't believe this shit. Keva and I finally got to the point where we were ready to let everybody know that we're together and Trinity pulls this shit. Hell naw! I got something for her ass.

I connected to my Bluetooth and called Lala. Her and her sister Kortni are my cousins and they always down to get into some shit for a couple hundred dollars. Lala answered and I ran down what I needed her and Kortni to do. As I thought, they were down for it and would let me know when it was done. Since I can't fuck Trinity up like I want to, Lala and Kortni gon' handle her ass for me.

Now let me figure out how to get my girl back!

Damarion

This shit with Keva is driving me out of my mind. I had no idea that she was this stubborn. I've sat outside of the door to her condo, slid letters under that same door, left flowers outside, sent flowers to her office, and sent emails. My last resort was to go to Kevan. I knew he wasn't fucking with me but I went ahead and threw that Hail Mary. I was relieved when he agreed to meet me for an early lunch today.

"Wassup," I said casually when I reached the table where he was sitting.

"Shit. You wanted to talk, so talk." I let out a deep breath before beginning.

"Look, Kev. First I want to apologize. I know I promised you I'd stay away from Keva and I did for as long as I could. Back then, I wasn't ready and it wouldn't have ended well. But years have passed, Bruh. I had all intentions of keeping my promise to you but shit happened and we couldn't fight it no more, man. I knew she had a nigga and I was cool with it 'cause that meant I could still do my dirt. After a few months, she felt guilty about sneaking around and wanted me to tell you. She was gonna end shit with Tyson but I was in denial about my feelings for her. Still scared to commit and shit. I realize now that I used the risk of losing our friendship as an excuse and we went our separate ways."

I took a breather and let my words sink in, hoping that he could see the sincerity in my eyes and hear it in my voice.

"What's changed?" he asked after a few moments of silence.

"Me."

"How, D? How have you changed? You act like a nigga ain't been around you on the regular. I see the shit you do with these women. What makes you think I would be cool with you doin' my sister like that?"

"Have you really been paying attention, Kev? Think about it. When was the last time you saw me out here wildin'? Or even heard me talkin' about fuckin' with a female."

"What about Trinity?" he asked after a few minutes.

"When I started dealing with Keva, I wasn't dealing with nobody else. Trinity and I started messing around shortly before that. The only reason I kept her around was because Keva had me in my feelings whenever Tyson was in town for extended periods. Trinity was just something to do and a way for me to convince myself that I wasn't in love with Keva. She was a distraction. We weren't in a relationship and just in case she was confused about it, I clarified it for her today."

The tension had lightened a bit but I could tell that Kevan was still on the fence about whether or not I had changed.

"You know, at the end of the day, I can't tell y'all what to do. Y'all grown. I appreciate you comin' through with the apology and letting me know what was up. My bad for comin' at you like that the other day but that shit blew me and I was mad as hell. You my brother, man. We good."

He stood and I did the same. We shook hands and exchanged a bro hug before I told him what I really needed from him.

"There's more and I need your help."

"Damn, man. We just got cool again and you already askin' for shit?" He laughed but when I didn't join him he stopped.

"Wassup," he said as he took his seat again. I did the same.

"You're gonna be an uncle."

He sat up and put his elbows on the table but didn't respond right away. I could tell from the expression on his face that he was processing what I'd said.

"Are you saying Keva is pregnant?"

"I am."

"By you?"

"Yup."

"How do you know it's not Tyson's?" As much as that question pissed me off, I can't be mad at the inquiry. It's legitimate.

"She says that it is and based on how far along she is, I believe her," I replied.

"Keva is my sister, I love her more than I love myself. But this...this situation...her behavior is just...," he looked off into space and didn't finish his statement.

Kevan would definitely be considered the 'good' twin of the two. Not to say that Keva is 'bad' but if you ask their parents, she was definitely more of a challenge for them when we were young. She goes against the grain any time the opportunity presents itself. Kevan has always been the one to walk the straight and narrow path so this situation with his twin doesn't sit well with him.

"I know but Keva has a good heart. This isn't the way she wanted things to be. I take some of the blame."

"What do you need my help with?" he asked because I still hadn't gotten around to that part yet.

"Trinity somehow got to Keva and told her that she was pregnant. Keva won't talk to me so I haven't had a chance to tell her that Trinity is lyin'."

"Is she lyin'?"

"Hell, yeah. I would never bless her with my seeds. Just help me get Keva to listen."

He sat back down and took a deep breath. "Aight, I'm gon' take your word on this shit. I gotchu."

Together, we concocted a plan for me to get my girl back.

Keva

The past two days have been hell trying to resist Damarion. With the way our relationship, or whatever it was, ended the first time, I was surprised by his persistence. He came to my condo on Tuesday and Wednesday and slid letters, which I have yet to read, under the door. When I opened the door today there were two bouquets of flowers waiting for me. I can't lie and say his efforts didn't put a smile on my face.

After working from home those two days, I had a meeting that I couldn't cancel and I had to go into the office today…Valentine's Day. Needless to say, I'm dreading interacting with people right now so I arrived at work thirty minutes before my meeting. When I opened the door to my office, I was blown away with what I saw. There were probably twelve bouquets of flowers, all different kinds, scattered through my office.

"Heather!" I screamed.

"Yes, Ms. Jamison," she replied as she rushed over to me.

"What's all this?"

"Umm, flowers, ma'am."

I looked at her through narrowed eyes. "I can see that Heather. Where did they come from?"

"Ms. Jamison, I would never disrespect your privacy by reading the cards. However, some of them came on Tuesday, some on Wednesday, and these over here, just this morning."

I took a deep breath and shook my head. "Okay. Thank you, Heather. I'll see you in the conference room for the one o'clock."

Heather went back to her desk and I went inside my office and closed the door. I know these flowers are from Damarion and I'll have to talk to him eventually. It's time for me to stop running and face the fact that the baby I'm carrying may not be the only one he has on the way.

The meeting went well and didn't last long because I came prepared. When I got back to my office I almost jumped out of my skin when I saw Kevan sitting at my desk.

"Shit, Kevan. You almost scared me to death! What are you doing here?"

I closed my door, leaned against it and folded my arms across my chest. Then I realized that doing that exposed my barely-there baby bump that seems to be growing by the minute. Instead, I took a seat at the small couch.

"I talked to D. He told me everything so you can stop trying to cover that little bump. Congratulations." Kevan got straight to the point, no beating around the bush.

"Oh…uhh…He did? Umm, thank you," I said hesitantly because I was caught a little off-guard.

"Are you sure it's D's baby? Cause you certainly got him convinced." *Ouch! That hurt!*

Not being able to look him in the eyes, I focused on my hands in my lap. "I guess I deserved that but yes I'm sure."

"Ke, when did we start lying to each other and hidin' shit?" I could hear the hurt in his voice and I shrugged my shoulders, not knowing what to say.

"I knew some shit was goin' on with you. Straight up, Sis, you been living foul as hell. If you weren't feeling Tyson like that, why string him along? To make matters worse, you accepted his proposal." He shook his head in disgust and I felt like utter shit.

"You're right, Kev. I'm a fucked up individual. There's no excuse," I cried.

"Why didn't you tell me?" he asked.

"Tell you what, Kevan? What was I supposed to say? Huh? Do you know how long Damarion and I fought our feelings for each other? Years, Kevan. We fought them for years! We only just acted on them recently. We ended it because of his loyalty to you…the promise he made you to not fuck with me. I didn't want to be the reason that eighteen years of friendship ended so I let him make the choice. He chose your friendship."

"First of all, that nigga didn't choose our friendship. He was just afraid to commit and he used that shit as an excuse. You're my sister, my got damn twin, and he's like a brother. I would've been pissed but I would've gotten over it. I've already gotten over it."

"Well, I'm glad you've gotten over it but it doesn't matter now. Damarion and I are over before we had a chance to get started."

"You need to talk to him."

"Why? I don't wanna deal with him and his baby mama drama for the rest of my life. She can have him and we can co-parent."

"This is the shit I was trying to keep you away from. I love D but I've never agreed with the way he handles women."

"Oh, this is your 'I told you so' moment. You---,"

"Shut up and let me finish, damn! The nigga came to me damn near in tears. He's different. Hear him out. He loves you and that girl ain't pregnant by him. If you would stop being so damn stubborn and hear the man out you'd know that already."

Kevan stood and I did the same. We walked to my office door and he pulled me into a hug. Putting his hand on the knob, he paused before turning it.

"It wasn't that I had a problem with y'all being together. I was trying to protect your heart and not have to beat my brother's ass. I love you, Sis." He kissed my cheek and left.

Trinity's not pregnant? That hoe was lying? I grabbed my phone, unblocked Damarion's number and called him. It went straight to voicemail. I called again and it did the same. *Shit!* Maybe he's ignoring me now. *Has he given up?* It makes me sick to even think that. *Isn't this what I've been asking for by ignoring him?* Well, yeah but that's not what I want. *What if I've ignored him for too long and now he's given up on me?*

This is turning out to be the worst Valentine's Day ever. Even when I was single with no prospects on the horizon I didn't feel as miserable as I do right now. I'm about to take my ass home, take off these clothes and go to bed. It's only three o'clock. I can get a good nap in and maybe later on I'll order take out and do some online shopping to make myself feel better. The sooner this day ends, the better!

****

Why me? It felt like I only closed my eyes five minutes ago. Now some idiot is pressing my buzzer like the damn building is on fire. I felt around my bed for my phone to check the time. *Shit!* I've only been asleep for forty-five minutes. I eased out of my bed and angrily stomped to see who has lost their natural mind.

Looking at the monitor to see who I was going to kill, Farrah came into view. I pressed the button so that she could hear me chew her out.

"Farrah, have you lost your ever-lovin' mind? Why are you laying on my buzzer like you're crazy?"

She looked at the monitor as if she could see me before yelling back at me.

"Keva, what the hell are you doing up there? I've been out here for twenty minutes waiting for you to answer. Why'd you change the code? Open the damn door. I have a bone to pick with you and I ain't doing it from here."

"Well, if you're only here to pick a bone, I don't' know if I want to let you in. Bye!" I laughed.

"Keva! Keva! You better not leave me out here." She pressed the buzzer repeatedly and I was bent over laughing as I watched her on the monitor.

"Fine! But you better not come in here on no bullshit." I buzzed her in and unlocked my door.

I sat on my couch and waited for Farrah to make her entrance. It's been a minute since we've gotten together and there is so much I've been keeping from her. I'm sure that since Damarion told Kevan everything, that Kevan told Farrah. Those two don't keep anything from each other which is why I've kept everything from her.

I heard a knock followed by the door opening. When I looked up, Farrah was locking the door and peeling out of her layers. She looked super cute in a red one-piece jumpsuit with leopard booties. I know she didn't get all dressed up to come bitch at me so she must be meeting Kevan somewhere later. It is Valentine's Day.

"There are some waters in the fridge if you want. Other than that, you're on your own. I need to go grocery shopping," I called out to her.

"I'm good. As much as I want to go off on you, there's no time for that. Go take a shower!" She demanded as she made her way over to me.

"Wait! What? Why do I need to shower?"

"Keva, you on my shit list right now. In the past hour, I found out that you've been having a secret affair with Damarion and supposedly pregnant with his baby and you broke up with Tyson. These are things that I should find out from you, my best friend, *not* my fiancé. I am not in the mood to go back and forth with you because I might hurt your feelings. Get in the shower!"

"What do you mean *supposedly*? This is Damarion's baby!"

"Yeah, yeah, yeah! If that's what you say. Get in the shower. I'm not gon' tell you again!"

Without any more objection, I went and got my ass in the shower. I don't know what the hell she has planned but I'll go along with it for now.

When I got out of the shower, Farrah was at my vanity table, pulling makeup from her huge makeup bag that I don't recall seeing when she came in. Although she has a career in finance, one of her hobbies is makeup application. She could probably do it full-time if she wasn't so fascinated with numbers.

"Okay. Tell me what you're doing here on Valentine's Day, of all days, forcing me to get dressed and apparently wear a pound of makeup. Why aren't you with my brother?"

Silence...

"Farrah, I know you're mad but the least you can do is tell me what I'm about to do."

"I'm not telling you anything. You owe me. Now sit down and let me fix your face," she demanded with her little attitude that I'm just about sick of.

"You don't have to be so damn rude. I'm sorry, okay. It wasn't my intention to not ever tell you but I know how you and Kevan pillow talk and this would have been too much for me to ask you to keep secret."

She looked at me in shock with her eyes wide and mouth agape. She started to speak, I'm sure to deny what I know is the truth but nothing came out.

"You know I'm right," I said.

"Knowing how Kevan feels...or felt about Damarion messing with his sister, it would have been hard as hell to not tell him. But you're my best friend, Ke. I knew you before I knew him. I want you to be able to talk to me and trust that I can keep your secrets. It would have been hard but I would never betray your trust."

Farrah is an emotional and sensitive being. Tears began to gather in her eyes and I went to her to give her a hug.

"Nobody knew about this. I wasn't proud of what I was doing. I'm not the cheating type, or at least I didn't think I was. And hurting Tyson was the last thing that I wanted to do."

"Ohhhh, poor Tyson. How'd he take it?" She asked when we pulled apart.

"Farrah, it broke my heart. And when I told him about the baby he lost it. He threw the vase I had on my coffee table against the wall. Then Damarion came out of the room---,"

"Hold up!" she interrupted. "You had Damarion here when you broke off the engagement to Tyson?" She shook her head in confusion.

"Damarion wouldn't leave. I made him promise to stay in my room but when he heard Tyson yelling and the vase shattering, he was out before the glass hit the floor," I explained.

"Wow. You got some shit goin' on around here."

"I know but I'm done with all this drama. I just hope the Lord forgives me for breaking Tyson's heart. Doesn't seem like it was worth it considering Damarion and I aren't even speaking. I finally called him today after ignoring him for a couple of days because Trinity came to my job talking about she's pregnant. Kevan told me that the hoe was lying but now Damarion won't take my calls."

"From what I understand, he's been trying to talk to you for the past couple of days. Maybe he's just giving you some space," she reasoned.

"But I don't want space anymore. I want my man back," I cried.

"Your ass is so damn stubborn and spoiled. You've been ignoring him for days and now that you've decided to stop, he's supposed to drop everything and come to you."

"Well...yeah."

"Girl, bye! Enough about all that. Sit down so I can get you ready."

"What am I getting ready for. It's Valentine's Day. You should be with Kevan."

"Don't worry about me," was all she said in return. I sat down and let her transform me. For what, I have no idea.

Keva

At some point, I stopped asking Farrah what was going on. She had my face looking flawless and picked out a floor-length red wrap dress that I had bought a few months ago for me to wear. I was accessorized with a gold necklace, earrings, and bangle bracelets. To finish my look off, I wore my gold shimmery stilettoes.

"Now can you tell me where we are going?" I asked as we walked to her car. Thankfully, the snow from the previous week had melted and I made it to her car safely.

"To the Four Seasons."

"The Four Seasons? What's there?"

She turned to look at me then rolled her eyes back to the road.

"Well, if you must know, your brother feels bad about something he said to you when he found out that you and D were messing around. He wants to make it up to you and since you and D aren't on the best terms right now and it's Valentine's Day, he convinced me to let you crash our plans."

Immediately tears gathered in my eyes and I covered my mouth as I gasped.

"Are you serious? He didn't have to do that. I don't want to mess up whatever y'all got goin' on," I reasoned.

"It's cool. All he wants to do is try to get me pregnant so I'll do anything to distract him from that at the moment."

"Are you sure, Farrah? I was perfectly cool with the plans I had by myself tonight."

"It's all good bestie and it's not like you or I have a choice. You know how Kevan is with you." She shook her head. Kevan can be a little overbearing when it comes to me. Always has been.

About ten minutes later we pulled into the parking garage at the Four Seasons in downtown Chicago. Once inside the hotel, I followed Farrah to the elevators.

"Where are we going? Aren't we eating at the restaurant down here?" I asked.

"Kevan's not answering my texts. We got a room for tonight, and yes, your ass is going home after we eat. He probably fell asleep."

We got off on the fortieth floor and she led the way to the room they had reserved. When we arrived she unlocked the door and pushed it open. Kevan had definitely fallen asleep because the whole suite was pitch black except the light from outside coming in through the window.

I could hear her feeling around on the wall for the light switch and when she turned it on, my knees got weak at the sight before me.

First of all, the living area of the suite was huge. There were red and white balloons floating throughout the room. Roses were strategically placed on the floor in the shape of a huge heart. In the middle of that heart was him...the love of my life. He was on one knee with a small Tiffany Blue box in his hand, looking handsome as ever.

He was wearing a black suit that I'm sure had to be tailored to fit his solid but lean physique. Underneath the suit jacket, he wore a red shirt that was decorated with black speckles. I know he chose to wear a bow-tie because I've told him many times that seeing him in bow-ties made my nipples hard and my pussy tingle.

"Oh my God! Is that---is this---are you---," I couldn't gather a coherent thought to put my words together.

"Sshhh…don't talk, just listen, baby. C'mere," he demanded.

Since Farrah turned on the lights my entire focus has been on Damarion. I took a deep breath and looked around the room, noticing my parents in one corner, Damarion's parents in the other, along with a photographer, and behind me stood my brother with Farrah. My eyes connected with Kevan's and he smiled and nodded towards Damarion. I slowly went to him as he held out one hand for me, holding the small box in other.

With our fingers intertwined, him looking up and into my eyes, he spoke the most beautiful words I've ever heard.

You are, the best part of me
My in between
My parts unseen
My intimacy – damn Keva
I never felt like this about anyone
Never cried or missed
Never lied or dissed
That's how I know you're the one
My nine to five, my late nights and morning after
My skin to skin, lip to lip moans and laughter
I tried to man up and act like it wasn't that serious
Tried to convince myself I didn't need to settle down
And my affection for you was temporary
But on the contrary, time away from you made me
Miserable and forced me to keep it real
Truth is, there's never been a woman who could make me
Commit to what I feel
That's how I know this shit is real
Our connection
Our affection
We were always meant to be
I love you, Keva

Will you marry me?

"Yes! Oh my God! Yes, baby! I will marry you!" I quickly accepted, barely allowing him to finish the question.

He opened the Tiffany Blue box and inside was a gorgeous ring. It looked to be about three carats and had a yellow square cut diamond in the middle. It was framed in white diamonds, including the band and when he slid it on my finger, I fell in love with it.

Just a few days ago, I was asked this same question by a man that was a temporary placeholder. Someone that did not make my heart smile, my pulse quicken, or my pussy thump. He was not who I was meant to be with because that man is now standing before me with so much love in his eyes. There is no doubt in my mind or heart that Damarion was made just for me. This has turned out to be the best Valentine's Day ever!

Damarion

S he said yes! Keva accepted my proposal. A nigga is high key on cloud nine right now. As soon as she agreed to be my wife, our mother's along with Farrah, whisked her off to another room. Keva didn't know then but I'm sure that she knows now that today is our wedding day. When I asked her to be my wife, I meant that shit and we will be getting married in a matter of hours. With the help of our parents, Kevan and Farrah, I was able to pull off a grand proposal. I'm praying that the wedding goes off without a hitch as well.

When I asked Kevan to help me get Keva back, he asked how serious I was about her. Without having to think about it, my reply was, "I want her to be my wife. I'd marry her today if I could." The look of surprise on Kevan's face was to be expected but it was important to me that he understood how serious I was.

His reply was, "Let's make that happen!"

At that point, I called my parent's and had them meet me at the Jamisons. Kevan also called Farrah and asked her to do the same. We needed all hands on deck to pull this off. The only problem was that no one knew that Keva and I were together so I had to update them. I decided I'd tell them about everything except the pregnancy since that may be something that Keva wanted to share. When we arrived, the five of them were in the den. From the look on their faces, I could see that they were concerned.

The conversation wasn't as hard as I thought it would be. Aunt Lisa, Kevan and Keva's mom, was upset that Keva led Tyson on all this time and accepted his proposal, knowing that she was in love with someone else. She said, "I liked Tyson because I thought Keva loved him and he's a nice young man. But for her to lead him on for all these months and her fast ass was screwing around with you behind his back…that's just not right. We didn't raise her like that."

Farrah was in her feelings about it all at first. Knowing that Keva kept all of this from her, being that they are best friends, made her feel some type of way. She vented to Kevan but once she got it all out, she was good. Thankfully, she didn't hold a grudge because she was a key factor in putting the proposal and wedding together. I would have loved to be a fly on the wall to see how their conversation went.

Apparently, my mom had some suspicions about Keva and I. When I came to her house in a funk the other day and used her phone to call Keva, her suspicions grew. She shared her thoughts with my father and he told her to mind her business. Uncle Rob, Kevan and Keva's father, didn't give a damn about nothing except his baby girl's happiness. He gave me his blessing right away. Everything fell into place perfectly and the icing on the cake was that my father was going to officiate our ceremony.

Now here I am, about to marry the woman that has made me want to be a better man. The woman that makes me feel like I can conquer anything that comes my way. The woman that wouldn't accept the crumbs that I was offering and made me want to man up and give her all of me. And God…I am so grateful.

Epilogue
~Valentine's Day 2020~

Keva

Today is the one year anniversary of our engagement and wedding. When Damarion proposed, I had no idea that he had also planned for us to get married that day as well. As soon as I said yes, I was whisked off to another room to get ready to marry the man of my dreams.

The wedding ceremony was small and intimate with only a few family members and friends, who, by the way, thought I was marrying Tyson up until they arrived. We all joke about it now but my life was a crazy ass mess a year ago on a Love and Hip Hop type of level.

After the ceremony, my mom had a few choice words for me. She was disappointed with how I handled everything and told me how lucky I was that Tyson wasn't crazy because he could have handled everything much worse, especially as far as the pregnancy was concerned.

Damarion and I welcomed our beautiful bouncing baby girl into the world at the end of August. Damaria Kevani is now five and a half months old and will be joined by hopefully a baby brother in seven months. Yes, Damarion's super sperm got me caught up again but I haven't told him yet. My plan is to surprise him tonight at dinner.

With that being said, we aren't doing a whole lot to celebrate our one year anniversary. Damarion wanted to go away for the weekend but I'm not ready to be away from Mari for that long yet. I agreed to one night so Damarion booked us a room at the Four Seasons downtown, which is where we were married, along with reservations at the Allium, the restaurant inside the hotel.

"Hey, baby. You good?" Damarion asked before he kissed my forehead.

"Yep. I just got Mari down for a nap. That girl knows she's a busy body. You check the mail?"

"Yeah, it's downstairs on the kitchen counter. Don't talk about my baby. She get that shit from her busy body mama anyway."

"Shut up!" I kissed his lips before leaving our bedroom to check the mail.

Damarion and I sold our condos and bought a house together in Lansing before I had Mari. It's about thirty minutes south of Chicago. Our parents would prefer that we were closer but we love it. Kevan and Farrah got married in October and are looking for a house near us. Farrah is finally giving Kevan some babies. She is pregnant with twins that had to be conceived on their honeymoon.

As I thumbed through the mail, I saw an envelope from the company I used to work for. Before having Mari, we decided that I wouldn't work outside the home for a few years. They did everything they could to convince me not to resign and they still call me at least three times a month to see if I've changed my mind. I haven't told Damarion yet but I'm thinking about doing some consulting for them and a few other companies.

I opened the manila envelope and inside of it was a smaller white envelope. When I pulled the white envelope out, I was shocked to see who it was from.

What the hell? Why would Tyson be writing me?

I haven't seen or spoken to Tyson since he left my condo the day I gave him the engagement ring back. We are still connected on social media and occasionally he will like a picture but we don't interact with each other.

I sat on one of the stools at the breakfast bar in our kitchen and opened the letter. Thinking about what he could possibly want to say to me had me feeling anxious.

Keva, I hope this letter finds you well. I'm sure you're wondering why I'm writing you so I won't beat around the bush. I wanted to let you know that I forgive you. I'm man enough to admit that you broke my heart and it's taken me awhile to get to a place where I could think of you without feeling angry. Once I got beyond the anger, I was able to reflect on our relationship. It was very one-sided. All the signs were there but I didn't want to accept the fact that my feelings for you were not reciprocated.

I also wanted to share something with you that I should have shared before I asked you to be my wife. Several years ago I found out that I am sterile and cannot have children. I apologize for demanding the DNA test. I knew that there was no chance of the baby being mine. At the time, I wanted to cause chaos and uncertainty in your life and that was wrong.

Anyway, I'm sure you haven't lost any sleep over me or our situation but you're a good person and I don't want you to feel guilty about following your heart...With Love, Tyson

As soon as Tyson found out that I had given birth, he went through the court system and demanded we get a DNA test. I've always known that Mari was Damarion's baby. There was never a doubt and if Damarion had any doubts he never shared them with me. So yeah, getting the DNA test did cause a little friction in my household.

All this time, what I did to Tyson...the way I did it, I did feel guilty about it. I can't say I lost any sleep but on the rare occasions that I thought of him, I felt bad.

Then this nigga tells me that he's sterile. So not only did he force me to get a DNA test on a child that he *knew* wasn't his, he proposed to me without disclosing the fact that he couldn't have children. Ain't that some shit!

Damarion

Sometimes I can't believe that I'm married. Other times, I can't believe that I'm married to Keva. Our first year of marriage has been better than I could have ever imagined. I don't like to think about what my life would be like without my wife and my baby girl. They are my world and I do all that I can to keep them smiling.

Since Keva refused to leave Mari for more than one night, I had to figure out a way to make our first anniversary special. Along with dinner at The Four Seasons, I had a few other things up my sleeve.

Keva is still nursing Mari so we decided to get dressed at home, allowing her to feed Mari before we left. I don't know if feeding her was supposed to make her breasts appear less full but it sure as hell didn't work. The black fitted dress that she was wearing had a deep neckline and her cleavage was damn near pouring out. It was hard to focus on the food and our conversation with her cleavage on display the way it was.

After dinner, we took the elevator up to our room on the fortieth floor. Keva had no idea that I had booked the same suite we had the night that I proposed and where we spent our first night as husband and wife. We held hands as we walked down the hall. She wasn't paying any attention because she was on the phone with her mom checking on Mari, which worked in my favor.

"Okay, Ma. I'll call a little later to see how she's doing."

"Keva, don't you call me again. If there's a problem, we will call you," Aunt Lisa yelled before she ended the call.

"Hello? Ma? Can you believe she hung up in my face?" she said in disbelief as she looked at the screen of her phone.

"Baby, Mari will be fine with our parents. She's in good hands. There are four of them and one of her. Relax."

We were standing right outside the room and she still hadn't noticed a thing. Her back was against the door and I stood in front of her with my arms locking her in place.

"I know, baby, but---," she started but was interrupted by my lips on top of hers.

We stood outside of the hotel room kissing like two teenagers for about five minutes until I couldn't stand the pressure of my dick trying to escape from my pants. I pulled away from her and looked into her eyes.

"Do you know how much I love you?" I asked even though I knew what her response would be.

"Yeah, but tell me anyway," she replied even though she knew what my response would be.

"To infinity and beyond, baby."

"I love you more."

"You ready to go inside?" I asked.

She nodded and I took her hand and brushed it against my hard dick.

"You sure about that?"

"Positive."

I unlocked the door and pushed it open, allowing Keva to enter first. I stood back so that I could see her reaction.

"Baby, is this our room?" She turned to look at me and I nodded. "Aww, baby. You are so sweet!"

She walked deeper into the suite and I heard her gasp before saying, "Oh my God! Baby, this is so beautiful!"

When she was about six months pregnant we had a maternity photo shoot on the beach. She had several pictures taken by herself and one picture in particular had me wanting to marry her ass all over again. In the picture, she was naked, sitting in the sand with her legs crossed in such a way that her intimate parts were covered and her hands were cupping her breasts. The sun reflecting off her skin made her look like an angel. I ain't never been a punk but that shit made me cry when I saw it. Deciding to get it enlarged and framed was probably more of a gift for me than her but she didn't have to know all that.

"You like it?"

"I love it! We can put it in the family room above the fireplace. Thank you, baby."

At this point, I was standing behind her with my arms around her waist as we both admired the picture.

"I have something for you too," she said and grabbed my hand to pull me into the bedroom.

As soon as she opened the door she saw the rose petals in the shape of a heart on the bed, along with the tray of chocolate covered strawberries with sparkling cider since she refused to drink any alcohol while nursing.

"Baby, when did you do this?"

"That's not important. I just want you to enjoy it," I told her as I guided her to the bathroom.

"But I didn't buy you anything big or expensive," she whined.

"I have you and Mari so I have everything I need." I kissed her forehead before opening the bathroom door and allowing her to enter first.

The jacuzzi tub was filled with water and rose petals. Candles were placed throughout the bathroom making it unnecessary to turn on the light.

"Baabyyy, you thought of everything," she squealed. "You gon' get all this good pussy tonight!" She did a little twerk against my dick.

"That was the plan all along, baby."

"Let's get in before the water gets cold." She turned around and pointed to her back, indicating that she needed me to unzip her.

She shimmied out of her dress, leaving her in just her bra and heels because she didn't have on any panties. *Shit!* Had I known that, dinner would have gone a little differently. I began taking off my clothes, anxious to be inside of her.

"Oh, wait. I need to get your gift. I'll be right back."

I watched her switch her sexy ass back into the bedroom and my dick throbbed thinking about what I was going to do to her tonight and into the wee hours of the morning, especially since we didn't have to worry about Mari waking her cockblocking ass up. I love my baby girl but I think she can sense when Daddy is about to get some pussy and her little ass be right up in the mix. When Keva returned, she had taken off her bra and heels and had her hands behind her back as she approached the tub where I was waiting for her.

"Whatcha got there?"

She put the rectangular shaped box on the edge of the tub and carefully stepped inside. Turning around, she eased her way down, resting her back against my chest.

"You just gon' tease me and put all that ass in my face like that."

"I'm not teasing you. You know you can have all this ass any time, any place."

She leaned her head against my shoulder, making it easier to plant kisses along her neck. I took complete advantage and got carried away, forgetting about my gift.

"Are you gonna open your gift?" she asked.

I lifted my head away from her neck and picked up the box. There was no wrapping paper just a bow around it which I untied and let fall to the floor then doing the same with the top to the box. When I saw what was inside the box, I looked at Keva, who had turned her body slightly and was looking at me anticipating my reaction.

"Hell naw! Is this for real, baby? You about to give me a son?"

"It's for real but I don't know about that son stuff. Are you happy?"

"Hell, yeah! This is the best gift you could ever give me." I kissed her lips hard. "How long have you known? Did you go to the doctor without me?"

"Of course not, baby. I just took the test a couple of days ago. I haven't even made an appointment yet," she reassured.

"Damn, baby. We fertile as hell. Mari only five months." I laughed.

"Yeah, I know," she said quietly.

"Aye, you okay with this? I mean, ain't shit we can do but how you feeling?"

"I feel fine. Just praying it's not twins." We both looked at each and then laughed.

"Damn, that would be crazy. Three kids under eighteen months." I shook my head at the thought but honestly, I'd love to have a set of twins.

I put the pregnancy test on the floor next to the tub before saying, "I want you to sit on this dick."

Without hesitating, she turned around and straddled me, slowly easing down. Once my full length was inside of her, she began to grind her hips in a circular motion. My tongue found her neck as she leaned her head to the side, allowing me full access.

As my wife's pussy gripped my dick, I thought about how I almost let her get away. It took another man trying to wife her for me to realize that I'd rather be with her than anyone else in this world. But I'd do it all again if it meant that I'd still end up right here, right now, releasing my seeds inside of this phenomenal ass pussy of the woman I love.

The End

Thank you for reading and I hope you enjoyed reading this Valentine's Day Novella. I appreciate your support and would love it if you could leave a review on Amazon and/or Goodreads.

You can find me at all of the following:

Reading Group: Kay Shanee's Reading Korner – After Dark
Facebook page: Author Kay Shanee
Instagram: @AuthorKayShanee
Goodreads: Kay Shanee
Subscribe to my mailing list: Subscribe to Kay Shanee
Website at www.AuthorKayShanee.com

Other books by Kay Shanee

Love Hate and Everything in Between

Love Doesn't Hurt

Love Unconventional

Completed Series

Until the Wheels Fall Off

Until the Wheels Fall Off…Again

Made in the USA
Middletown, DE
10 December 2023

45105796R00050